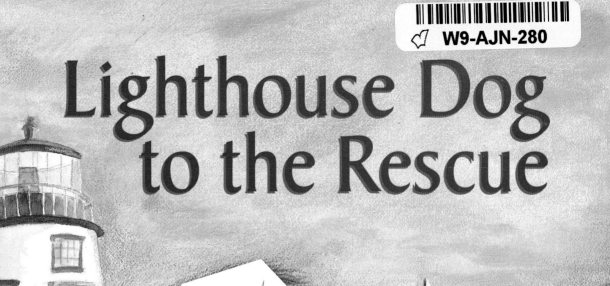

# Lighthouse Dog
## to the Rescue

By ANGELI PERROW / Pictures by EMILY HARRIS

DOWN EAST BOOKS

Story © 2000 by Angeli Perrow. Illustrations © 2000 by Emily Harris.
Printed in China
Down East Books / Rockport, Maine
Book orders: 1-800-766-1670
www.downeastbooks.com

ISBN: 0-89272-600-8

Library of Congress Control Number: 2002114599

IN MEMORY OF MY MOTHER.
ELSIE ROGERS SAVAGE,
WHO ROAMED IN HER GIRLHOOD
WITH SPANIELS FRECKLES AND BIG BOY.

Spot sat at the foot of the tower of Owls Head Light. It was the perfect lookout for a lighthouse dog. Ships and boats of many kinds passed by, and the friendly spaniel loved them all.

Across the gray water of Penobscot Bay, a bank of
fog was rolling in. Fog meant danger for ships. Spot barked
a warning.

Nearby played the lighthouse girls.
Pauline and her little sister, Millie, were sorting sea glass
into piles of pale green, emerald green, cobalt blue, root beer
brown, and milky white. When Pauline heard Spot bark, she
lifted her head and saw the fog creeping closer and closer.
"We must tell father!" she said to Millie.

They raced down the walkway to the house, where their father was painting the trim a bright white. Keeper Gus Hamor worked hard to keep the lighthouse station shipshape.

"Fog's coming in!" Pauline called to her father.

Keeper Hamor pulled on his jacket and fastened the brass buttons. Already, fingers of fog were curling around the lighthouse.

"It's going to be a pea-souper," he announced.

He sent Millie to the house for sandwiches. He and Pauline climbed the spiral staircase of the tower.

In the lantern room, Pauline and Spot watched as her father lit the lamp. It was a powerful light, but it did not shine far in the thick fog. "We will have to ring the bell," said Keeper Hamor.

Down the path they hurried. Pauline and her father took turns
pulling on the rope every few minutes. *Clang! Clang!* The sound of
the bell would guide the sailors even
if the light could not be seen.

Millie arrived with lunch. "Chicken sandwiches and tea!" she declared, smacking her lips.

Spot had been watching. Suddenly, he grabbed the rope with his teeth and backed up. The big bell pealed! His family was amazed.

"Smart dog!" Pauline praised her pet.

Spot was thrilled with his new skill. From that day on, every time a boat passed, he pulled on the rope to say hello.

*Clang! Clang! Clang!* the bell would sound, until the captain of the passing boat said, "Enough!" and rang his own bell in reply. Then the spaniel would rush to the water's edge and bark in delight. Before long, all the sailors of Penobscot Bay knew Spot, the lighthouse dog.

Captain Stuart Ames was especially fond of Spot. Twice a day his mailboat steamed past the lighthouse, carrying mail between Rockland and Matinicus Island. He welcomed the little dog's greeting. The captain was always sure to blow the boat's whistle and wave.

Often, in the afternoon, Mrs. Ames would call the Hamors at the lighthouse. "Have you seen the mailboat go by yet?" she would ask. If the answer was yes, she knew that Captain Ames was almost home, and it was time to start cooking his dinner.

Spot loved the life of a lighthouse dog. Through all seasons of the year, he greeted the passing boats.

Winter meant more work for the Hamor family. Day after day, they shoveled snow to clear the paths to the tower and bell.

One day, a blizzard hit the coast of Maine. Blinding snow swirled over Owls Head, and wind howled around the corners of the keeper's house.

Pauline and Millie were huddled on the rug playing paper dolls when their father put on his heavy overcoat and went out to check the light. Pauline wished he did not have to go out in such awful weather. She pressed her face to the window.

The yellow glow of his lantern soon disappeared in the storm.

Keeper Hamor clung to the slippery catwalk of the tower and scraped ice off the windows. Still, the lighthouse beam barely showed through the thick curtain of snow.

He trudged down the path to the bell. When he saw it, he was horrified. Sea spray had dashed against it, adding layer upon layer of ice. The bell was frozen solid!

Back at the house, the keeper sadly told his family, "Our light and our bell will not be guiding ships tonight." Pauline hoped all the sailors were safely home by now.

Just then the telephone rang. It was Mrs. Ames, and she sounded worried. "Captain Ames is two hours overdue. I'm afraid he has lost his way in the blizzard!"

"There has been no sign of the mailboat," Pauline's father answered, "but we might have missed it in the noise of the storm."

"My husband speaks often of your clever dog," said Mrs. Ames. "Do you think Spot might be able to hear the boat's whistle?"

Keeper Hamor gazed at Spot, who was dozing by the fire. "We will send him out and see what happens."

Pauline wrapped her arms around the dog's neck. "Spot," she said softly. "Listen for the mailboat. Captain Ames needs you."

Spot stood in the raging storm, listening and listening. He could hear nothing except the screaming wind and the pounding waves.

Finally, after half an hour, he scratched at the door to be let in.

"Poor thing!" exclaimed Pauline.

The dog's fur was crusted with ice. He lay down in an unhappy heap and closed his eyes. A puddle began to form around him.

Pauline wished there was something they could do to help Captain Ames. She hated to think of the mailboat tossing around in the wild waves, not knowing which way to go. Worst of all, what if it crashed on the rocks, as so many other boats had done in past storms?

After resting a few minutes, Spot suddenly sat up, alert and
listening. He scampered to the hall and barked to be let outside.
Pauline and her father threw on their coats and followed.

Spot struggled through the snow toward the fog bell, but the drifts were too deep. So he skirted the cliff top, which was blown clean by the wind. There he stopped and barked loudly. Again and again he barked.

Pauline peered over the cliff, but saw only whirling snow. She cupped her hand behind her ear and listened for the sound of a boat's engine, but all she heard was the roar of the storm. She wondered how Spot could possibly hear the mailboat.

But Spot did hear something. He stared out to sea—barking, then listening, then barking some more.

Then—yes! Pauline could hear it, too. There was the familiar whistle—three distant blasts to say that Captain Ames had heard Spot's barking!

Now the Captain knew where he was. He could chart a sure course for Rockland Harbor and home.

"You saved the day, Spot!" said the dog's proud mistress.

Two hours later, the Hamors' telephone rang again. It was Mrs. Ames. "Captain Ames is safely home, thanks to Spot," she announced. "Give that dear dog of yours a special treat tonight."

But Spot was already enjoying his reward. Pauline had toweled him dry, and Millie had made a bed for him by the fire. He was now munching on the biggest bone the girls had been able to find in the kitchen.

The spunky spaniel did not think of himself as a hero. Rescuing a friend was all in the line of duty for a lighthouse dog.

*A springer spaniel named Spot really did live at Owls Head lighthouse, in Maine, in the 1930s. He was the pet of Pauline Hamor, whose father was the keeper of the lighthouse.*

*Spot seems to have taken to the life of a lighthouse dog. He loved to ring the fog bell, which he learned to do by watching Keeper Hamor. Just as it was told in the story, Spot watched for passing boats to greet with the bell and a bark. The sailors of Penobscot Bay responded by blowing their boat whistles or fog horns.*

*After she was grown up, Pauline described the mailboat rescue to author Edward Rowe Snow, who wrote about it in his book,* The Lighthouses of New England.

*When Spot died, he was buried near the old fog bell he had loved so much.*